Emma's Christmas

an old song re-sung & pictured by
Irene Trivas

ORCHARD BOOKS · NEW YORK

Text and illustrations copyright © 1988 by Irene Trivas. All rights reserved. No part of this book may be reproduced or transmitted in any form or by any means, electronic or mechanical, including photocopying, recording or by any information storage or retrieval system, without permission in writing from the Publisher.

Orchard Books, 387 Park Avenue South, New York, New York 10016.

Manufactured in the United States of America   Book design by Mina Greenstein   10   9   8   7   6   5   4   3
The text of this book is set in 16 pt. Galliard. The illustrations are watercolor, reproduced in halftone

Library of Congress Cataloging-in-Publication Data.   Trivas, Irene. Emma's Christmas. "A Richard Jackson book."
Summary: A farm girl is courted by a prince who presents her with the gifts of the twelve days of Christmas, finally winning her and moving to the farm. [1. Christmas—Fiction.   2. Twelve days of Christmas (English folk song)—Adaptations]   I. Title.
PZ7.T7375Em   1988   [E]   88-1640   ISBN 0-531-05780-1   ISBN 0-531-08380-2 (lib. bdg.)

for JEAN MARZOLLO

Once upon a time, there was a farmer's daughter named Emma who went barefoot in the summer, talked to the pigs, and liked to sit in the branches of the old cherry tree all year round. She did wear boots in the winter.

On the first day of Christmas, the young local prince saw Emma in her tree. There and then he knew that she—and only she—could be his own true love.

The prince asked the farmer for Emma's hand in marriage. The farmer asked her how she felt about such an honor. Emma wasn't all that thrilled. The prince had a funny smile, and he was, to be sure, a prince. But she couldn't imagine herself living happily in a castle. "No," she said. "But thank you, Prince."

However, the prince would not take no for an answer.
Instead, that very day, he sent her by royal messenger…
a partridge in a pear tree.
Emma was pleasantly surprised.

On the second day of Christmas, two messengers
came bearing a cage with two turtle doves and another
partridge in another pear tree.
Emma was charmed.

On the morning of the third day of Christmas, three
men trudged through the snow with three French hens,
two more turtle doves, and a third partridge in a third
pear tree.

"He's overdoing it," muttered Emma's mother.

On the fourth day of Christmas, more messengers brought four calling birds who called out EMMA! EMMA! EMMA! EMMA! three French hens, two turtle doves, and another pear tree with yet another partridge.

"We'd better build a birdhouse," said Emma's father. Her mother made ten quarts of pear jam.

On the fifth day of Christmas, Emma received four
more calling birds, three more French hens, two more
turtle doves, another partridge in a pear tree and—for a
change—five golden rings.

At dawn on the sixth day of Christmas, Emma was still
in bed when she heard six knocks at the cottage door.
She peeked out the window and saw six swans
swimming in a silver pool. All the other birds
were stacked up by the chimney. Five more golden rings
were tied to the door handle.

KNOCK,
    KNOCK,
KNOCK,
     KNOCK,
KNOCK,
    KNOCK,
KNOCK.
It was the seventh day of Christmas.

When she opened the door, Emma saw seven geese
a-laying, six more swans a-swimming, five golden rings,
four calling birds, three French hens, two turtle doves,
and *another* partridge in a pear tree.

"That makes 69 birds…and they're all laying
eggs," she groaned.

On the eighth day of Christmas, there was something new: eight milking maids, each with her own pail, milking stool, and cow. Behind them were seven more geese, six more swimming swans, four calling birds, three French hens, and two turtle doves. Four more golden rings were hanging on the pear tree. A partridge was chewing on the fifth.

Worn out, Emma dreamed she heard music.
But it was no dream.

It was the morning of the ninth day of Christmas, and what she heard were nine pipers piping a tune that was so lovely she could almost ignore the eight new milkmaids and their cows, the seven new geese, the six new swans, the five new golden rings, the four new calling birds, three new French hens, two new turtle doves, and—way off in the distance—the partridge in the pear tree. But not quite.

On the tenth day of Christmas, the cottage door flew open, and ten drummers drummed their way inside to the nine pipers' piping. The eight milkmaids tumbled after with all the cows, geese, swans, golden rings, calling birds, French hens, turtle doves, and, of course, a partridge in *another* pear tree.

The farmer and his wife packed some eggs and one hundred jars of pear jam and left home to visit the farmer's ancient parents who lived far away on the other side of the kingdom. Emma stayed home to watch over the farm.

That night she made 52 pear omelettes for all the drummers, pipers, and maids. She fed the cows 24 bales of hay. The birds did very well on chopped pears and cottage cheese.

On the eleventh day of Christmas, eleven ladies danced in with ten more drummers, nine more pipers, eight more milking maids, and all the usual birds.

Emma made 90 omelettes, squeezed 10 gallons of pear juice, and fed everybody. Then she threw the 35 rings at the 32 calling birds, who were driving her crazy, screeching EMMA! EMMA! EMMA! EMMA!

On the twelfth day of Christmas a very weary Emma climbed up to the hayloft for some sleep.

But over the snowy hills she saw: twelve leaping lords, eleven dancing ladies, ten drumming drummers, nine piping pipers, eight milkmaids with cows, seven laying geese, six swimming swans, five pages bearing five golden rings, four calling birds, three French hens, two turtle doves, and—just behind the pear tree and its partridge—the prince himself, smiling his funny smile.

In spite of herself, Emma was enchanted.

The prince ran into the house and up the ladder. "Emma, my own true love!" he cried. "Now, will you be my princess and live with me in the castle?"

"Prince dear…yes and no," Emma replied. "I've
been thinking. Most of the castle's people must be
here by now. If they stayed, and you stayed…well,
then we could be married….Would you like to be my
Farmer Prince?"

"I'd love it," he said.

And so it was that Emma and the prince, in the company of 12 lords, 22 ladies, 30 drummers, 36 pipers, 40 milking maids and their cows, 42 geese, 42 swans, 36 calling birds, 30 French hens, 22 turtle doves, 12 partridges, and Emma's father and mother, exchanged 40 golden rings and were very happily married.

The pear trees grew into an orchard and the cows into a dairy herd. And the 184 birds laid thousands and thousands of eggs…

…most of which hatched.